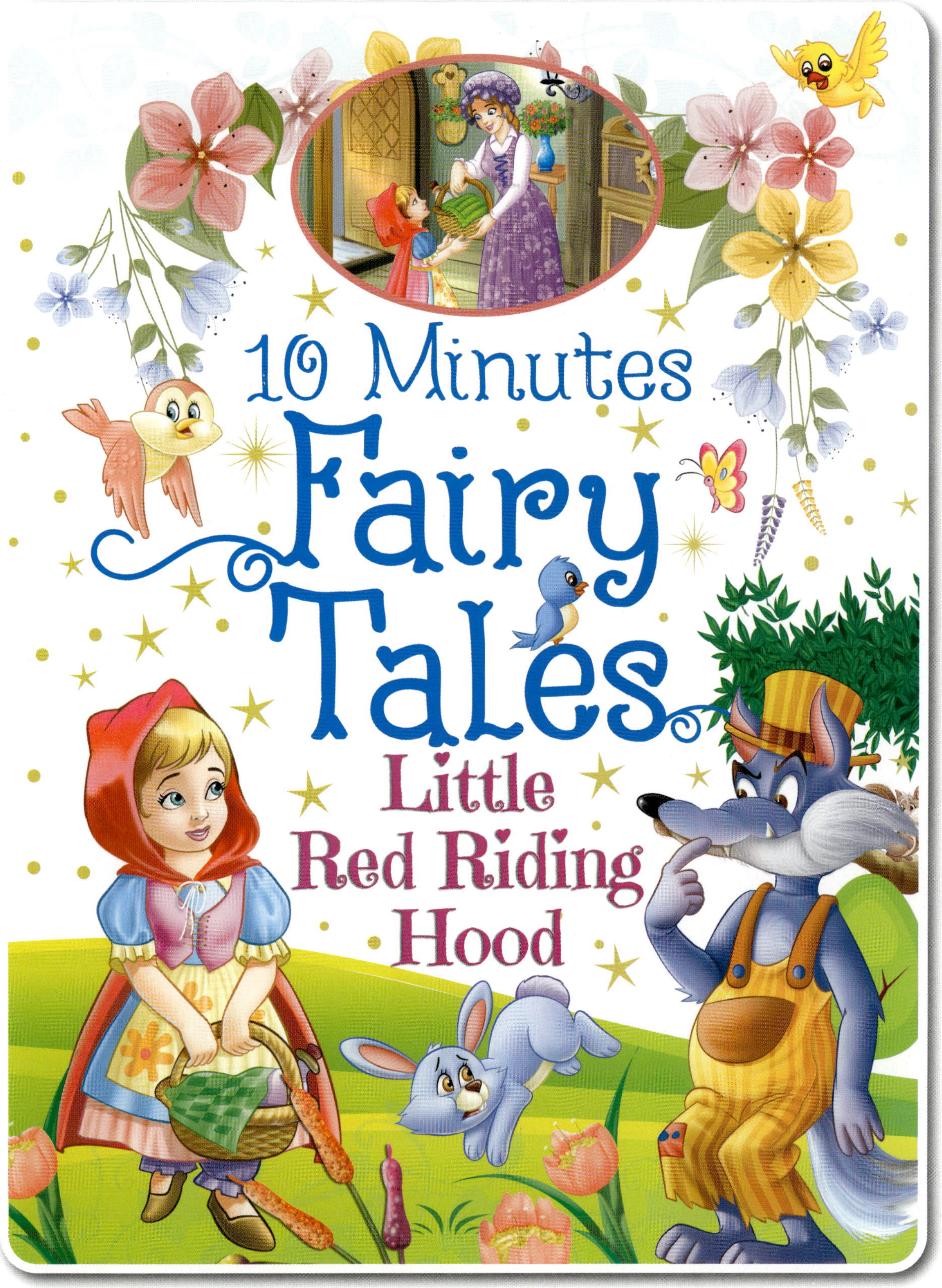
10 Minutes
Fairy Tales
Little
Red Riding
Hood

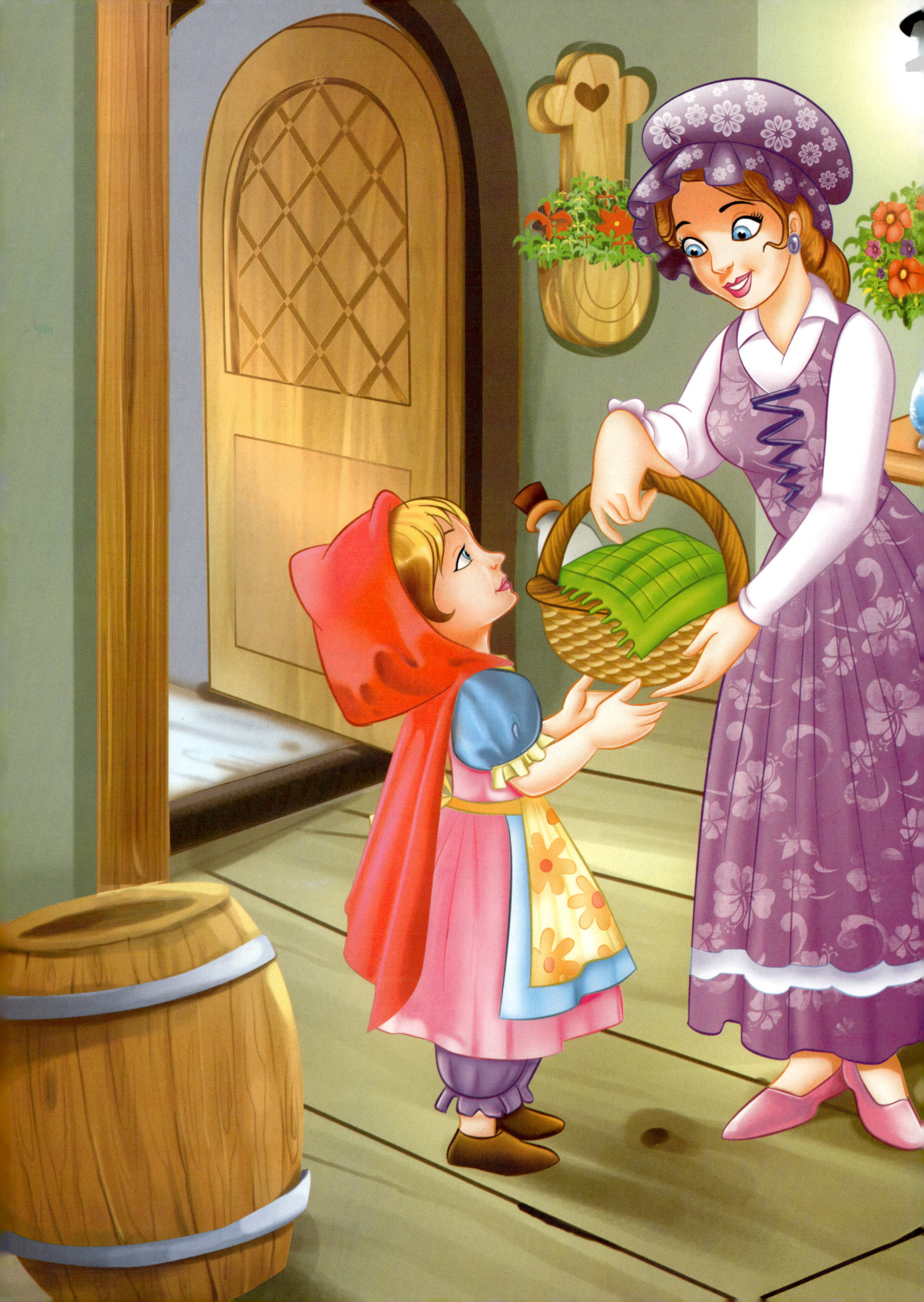

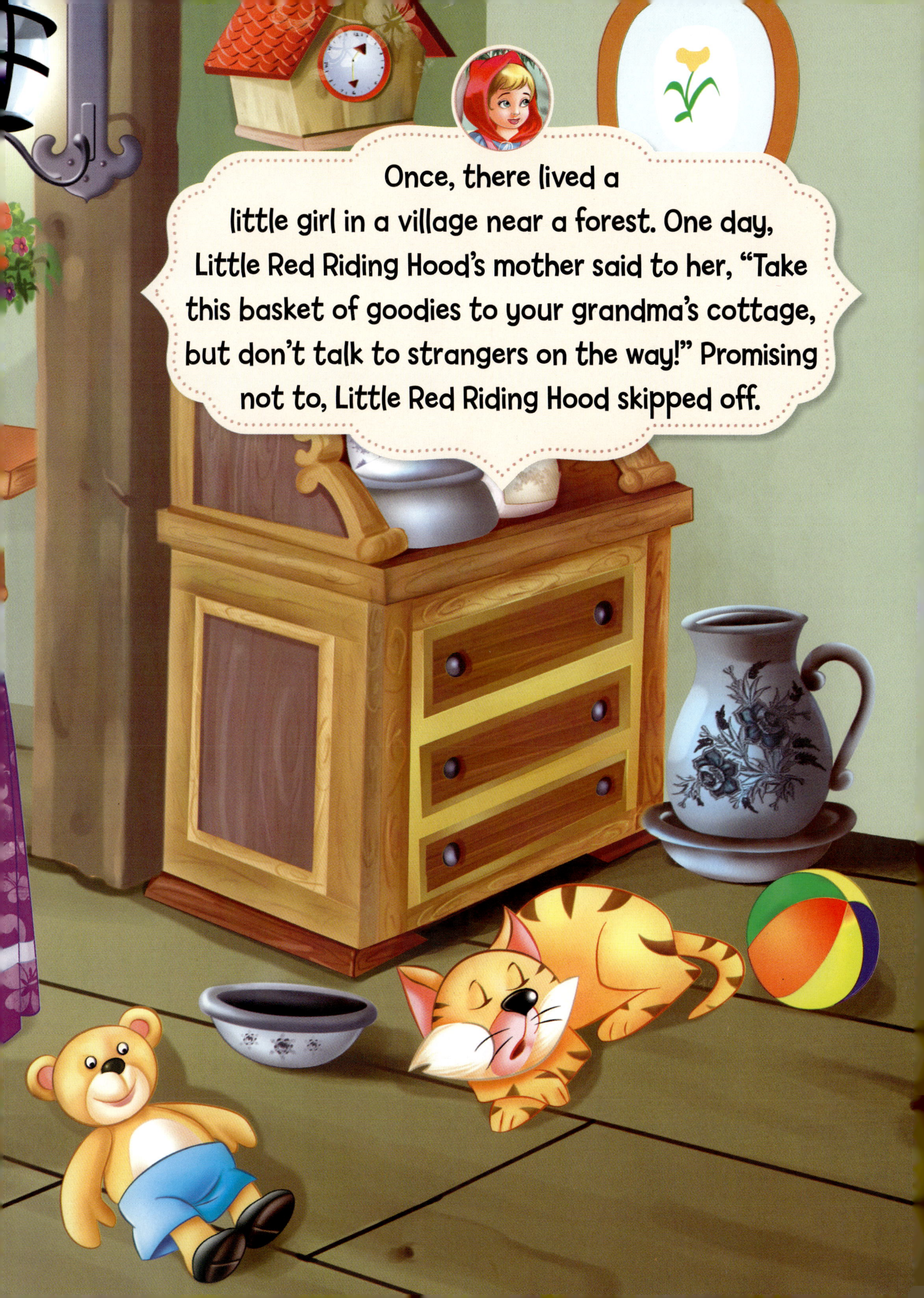

Once, there lived a little girl in a village near a forest. One day, Little Red Riding Hood's mother said to her, "Take this basket of goodies to your grandma's cottage, but don't talk to strangers on the way!" Promising not to, Little Red Riding Hood skipped off.

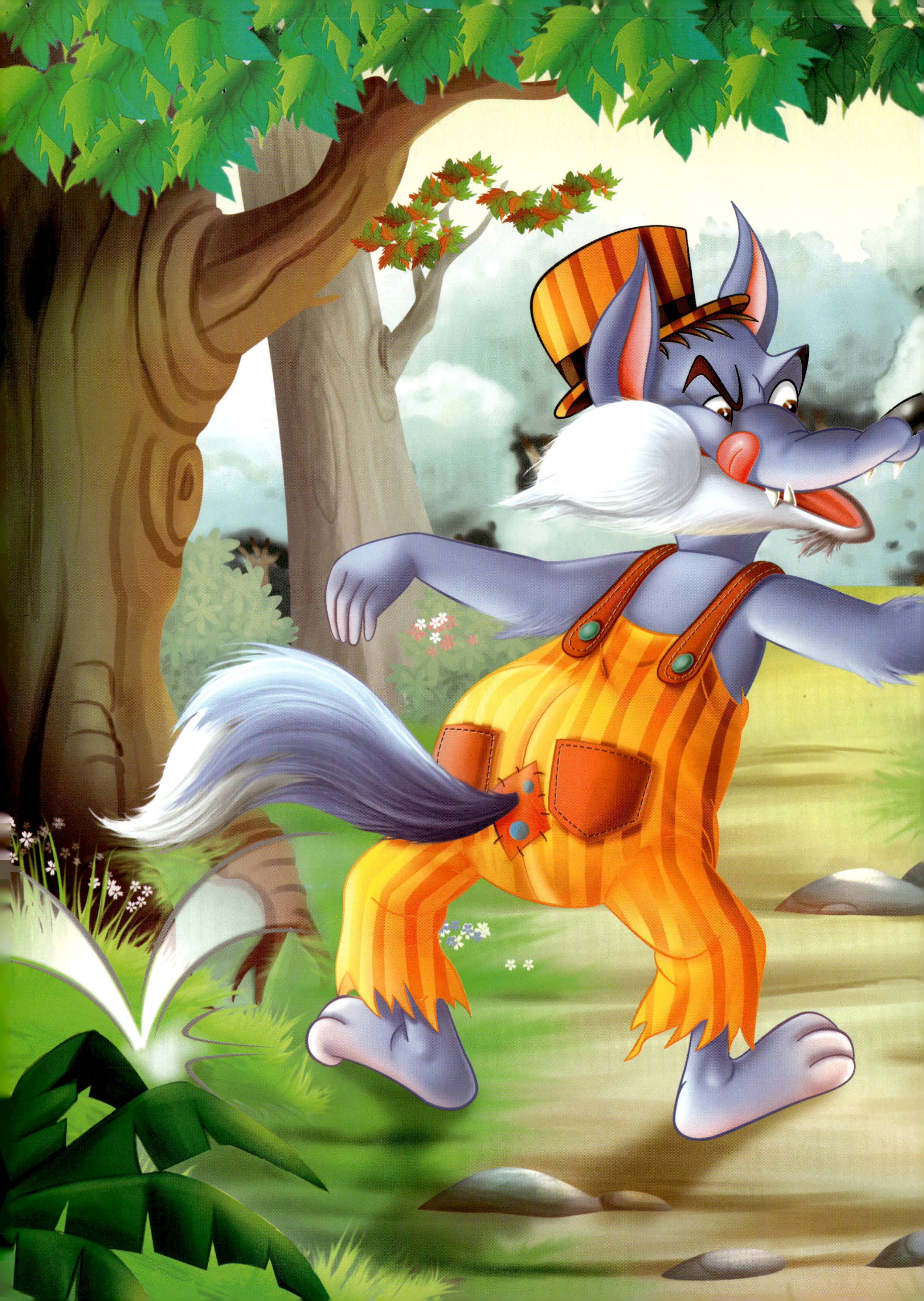

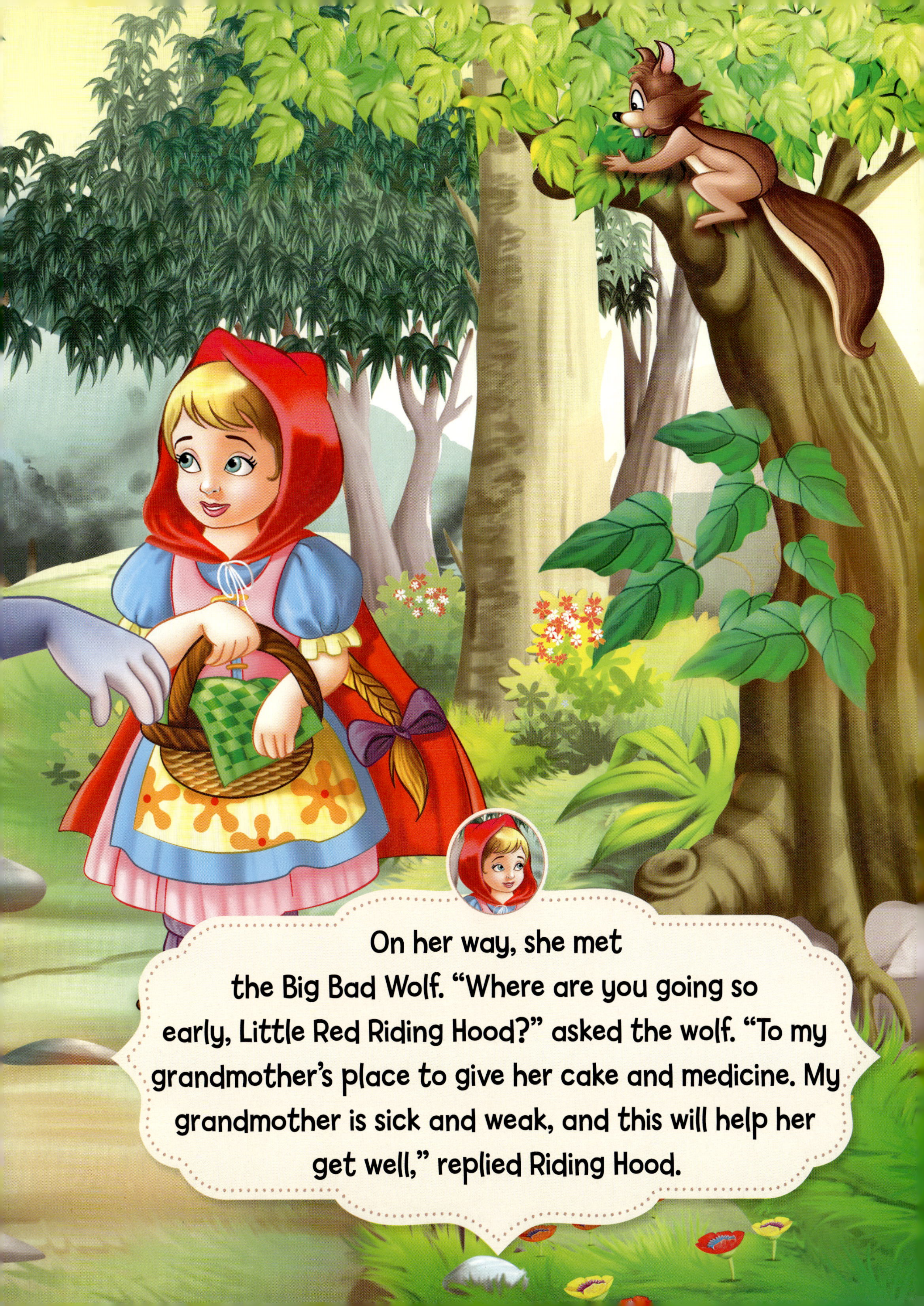

On her way, she met
the Big Bad Wolf. “Where are you going so
early, Little Red Riding Hood?” asked the wolf. “To my
grandmother’s place to give her cake and medicine. My
grandmother is sick and weak, and this will help her
get well,” replied Riding Hood.

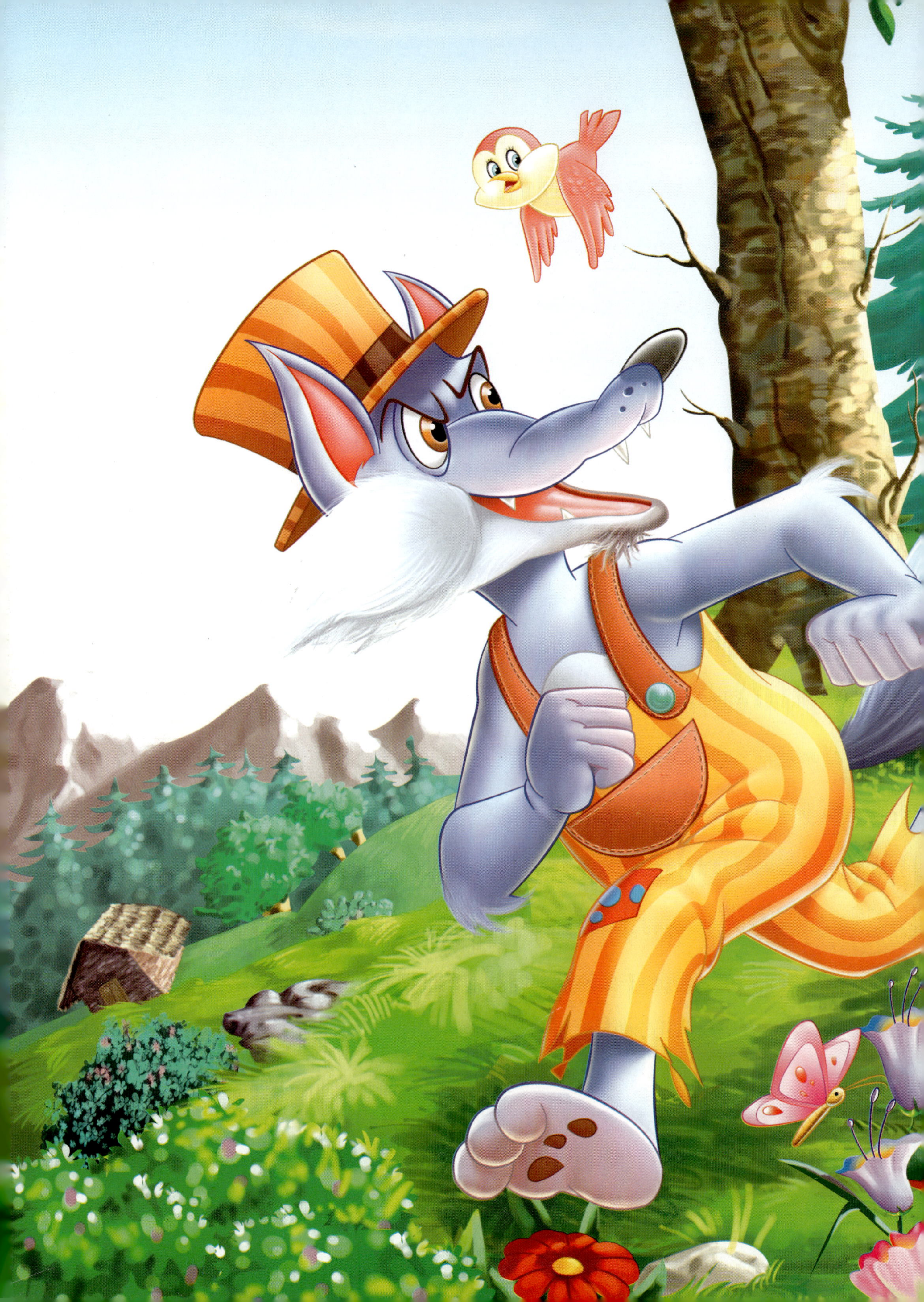

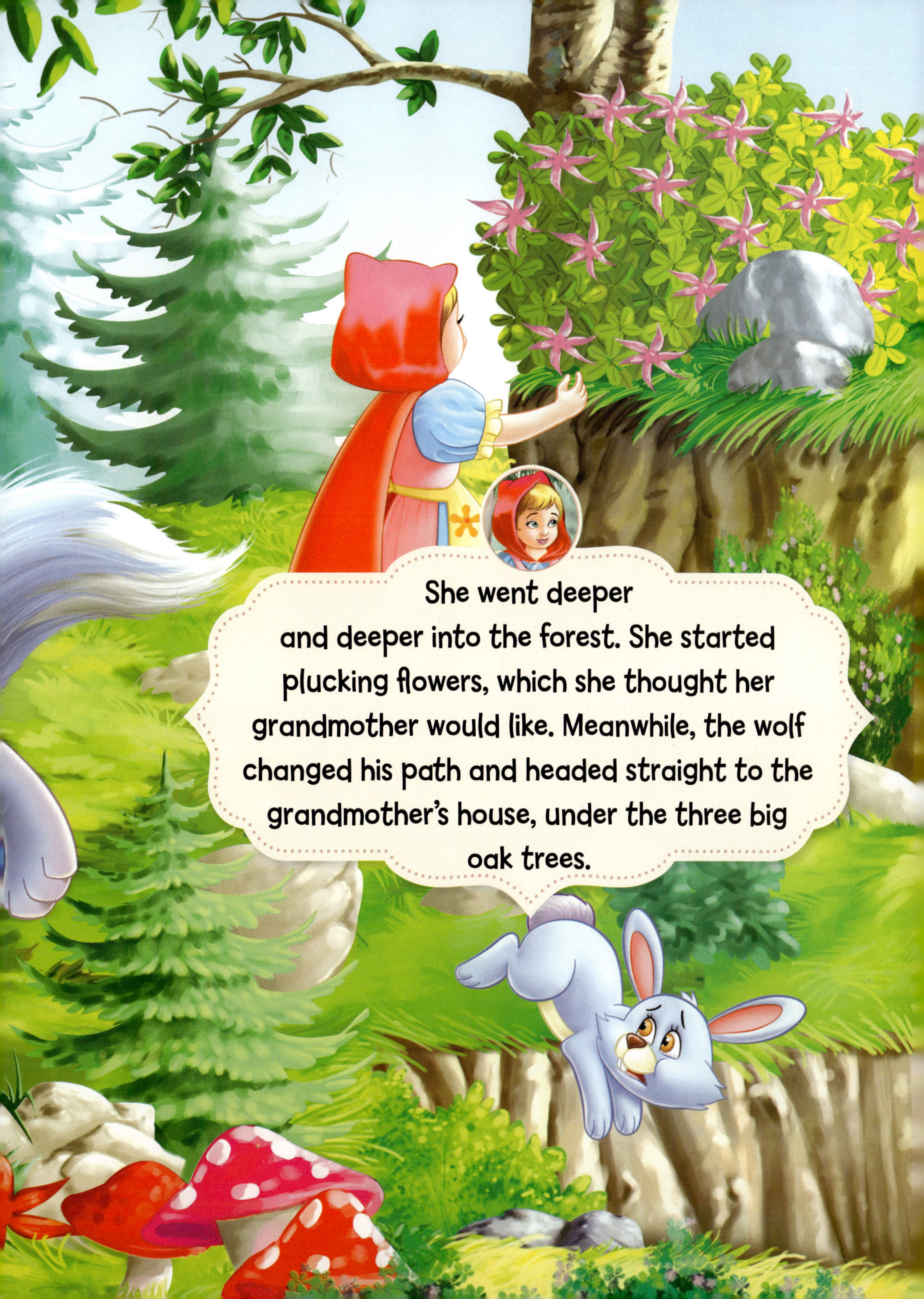

She went deeper
and deeper into the forest. She started plucking flowers, which she thought her grandmother would like. Meanwhile, the wolf changed his path and headed straight to the grandmother's house, under the three big oak trees.

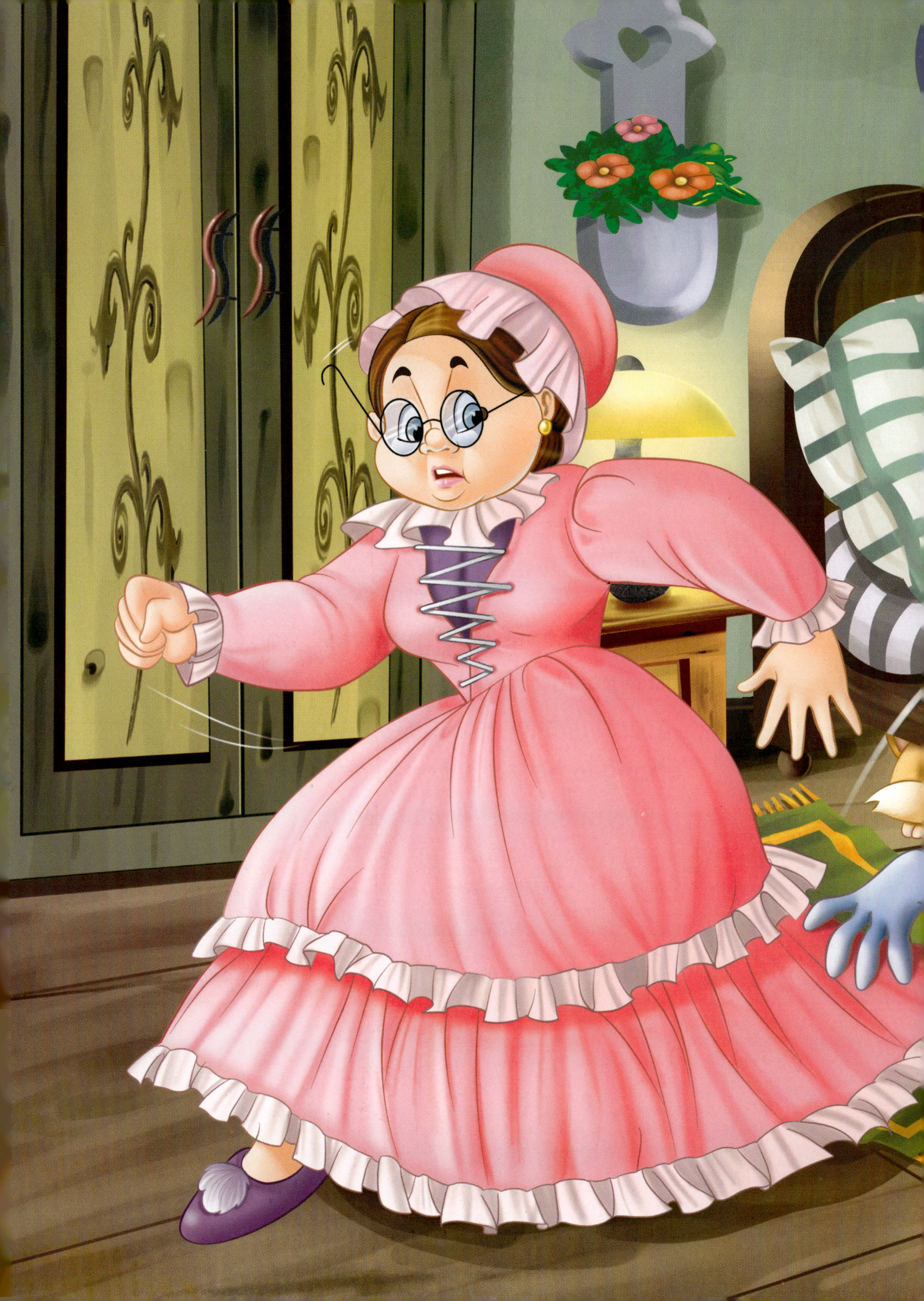

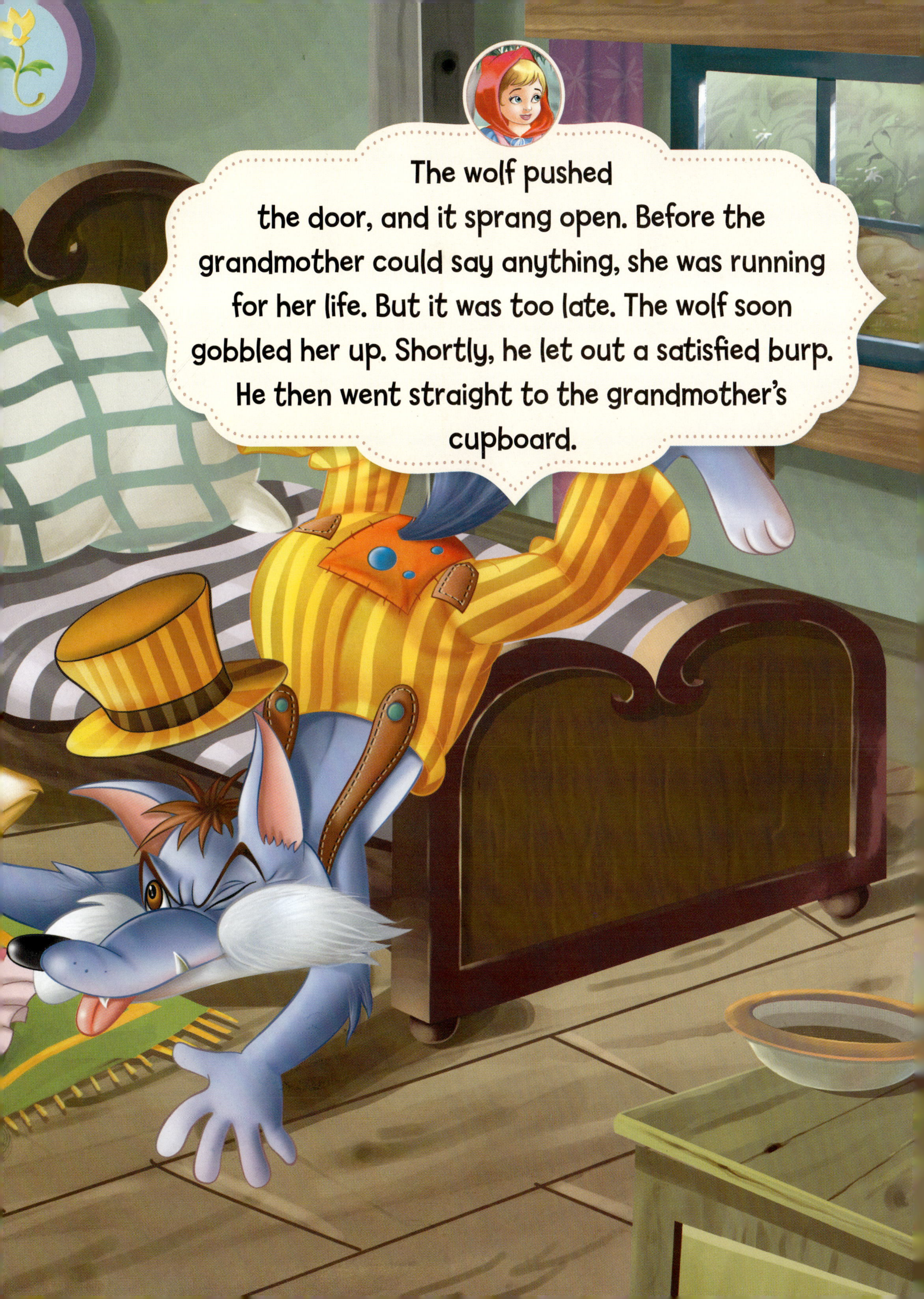

The wolf pushed the door, and it sprang open. Before the grandmother could say anything, she was running for her life. But it was too late. The wolf soon gobbled her up. Shortly, he let out a satisfied burp. He then went straight to the grandmother's cupboard.

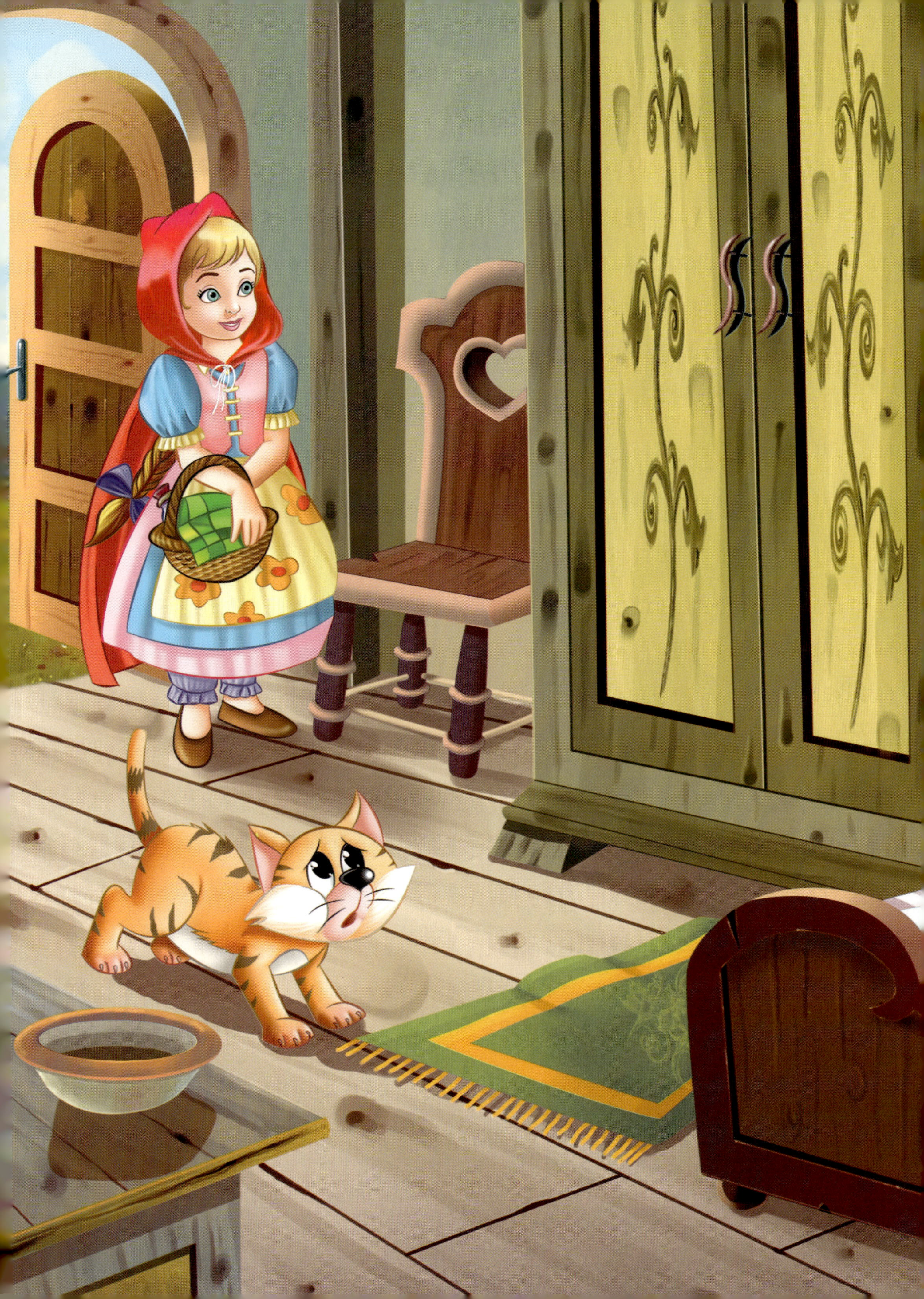

He turned his
back towards the door and pretended to sleep. Shortly, Red Riding Hood reached her grandmother's house. She was puzzled when she found the door open. She called out, "Good morning!" But she received no answer.

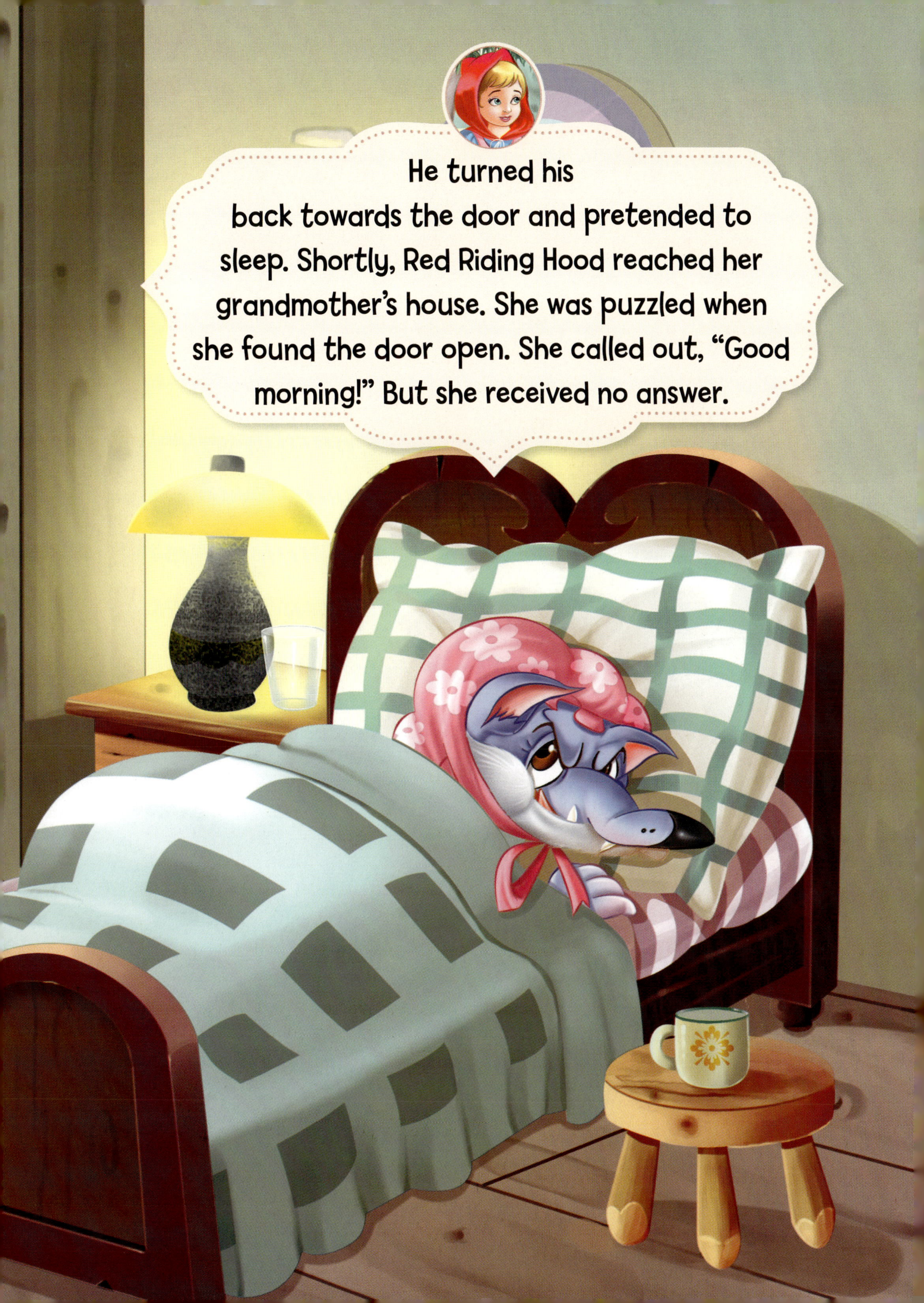

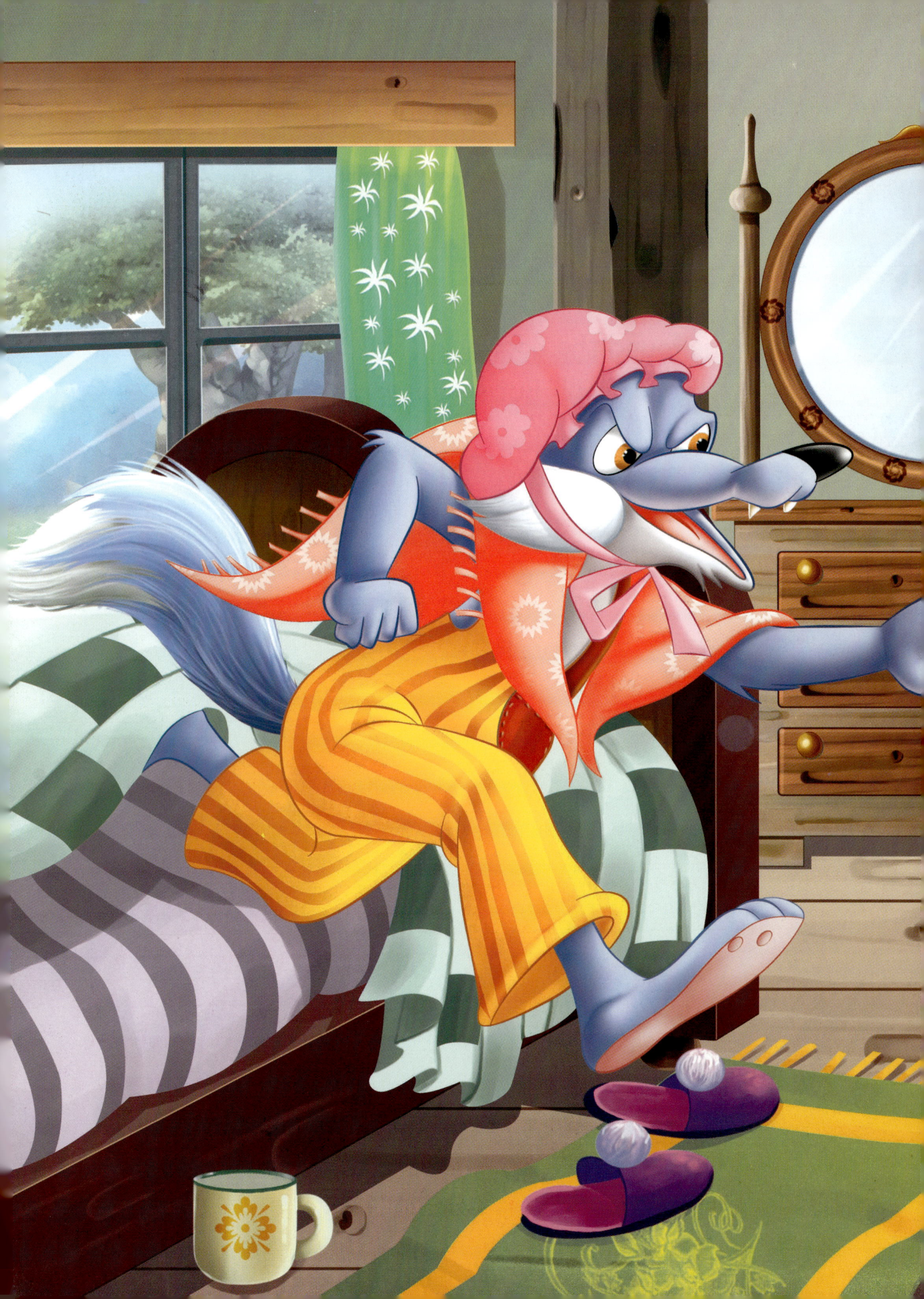

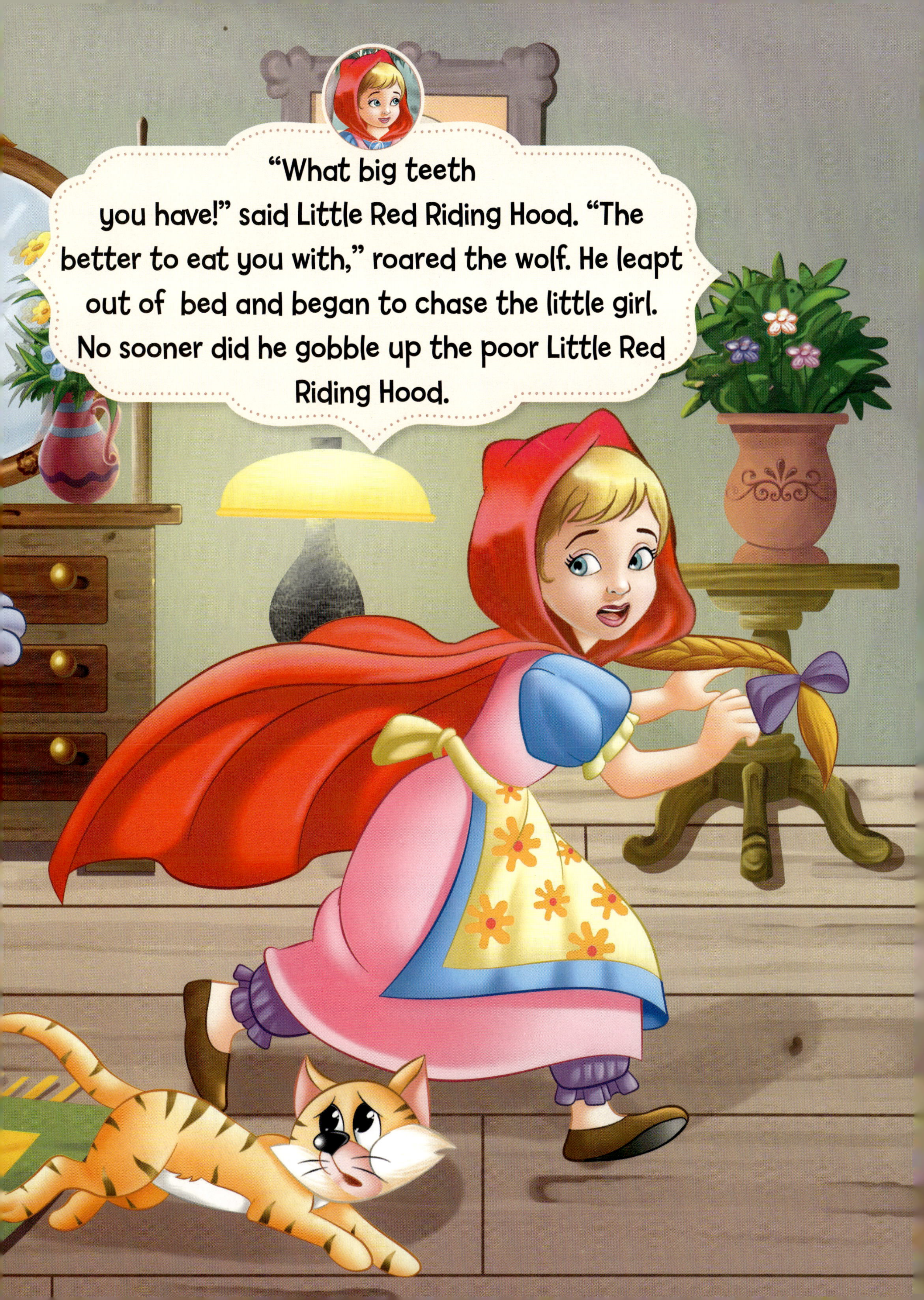
"What big teeth you have!" said Little Red Riding Hood. "The better to eat you with," roared the wolf. He leapt out of bed and began to chase the little girl. No sooner did he gobble up the poor Little Red Riding Hood.

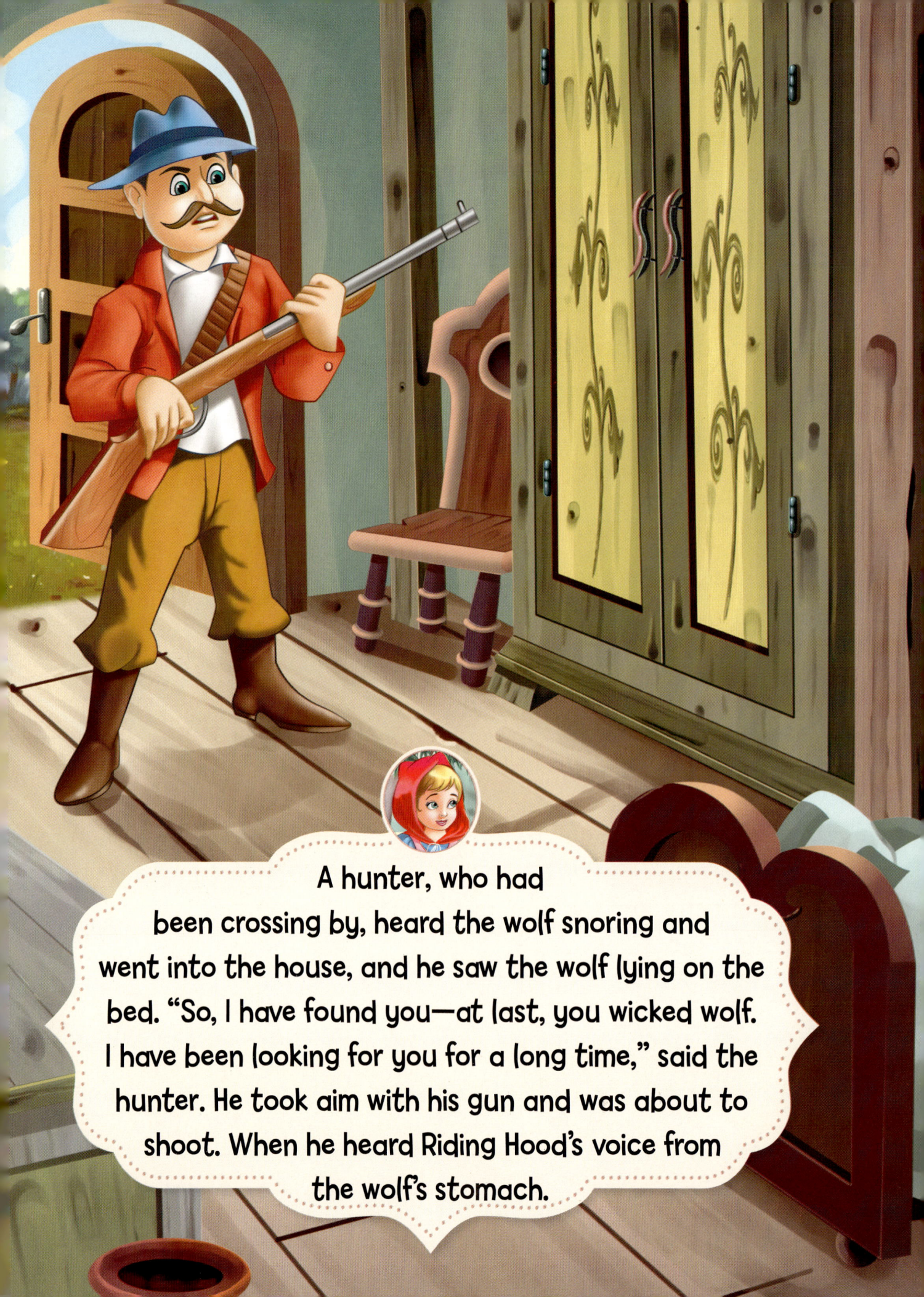

A hunter, who had been crossing by, heard the wolf snoring and went into the house, and he saw the wolf lying on the bed. "So, I have found you—at last, you wicked wolf. I have been looking for you for a long time," said the hunter. He took aim with his gun and was about to shoot. When he heard Riding Hood's voice from the wolf's stomach.

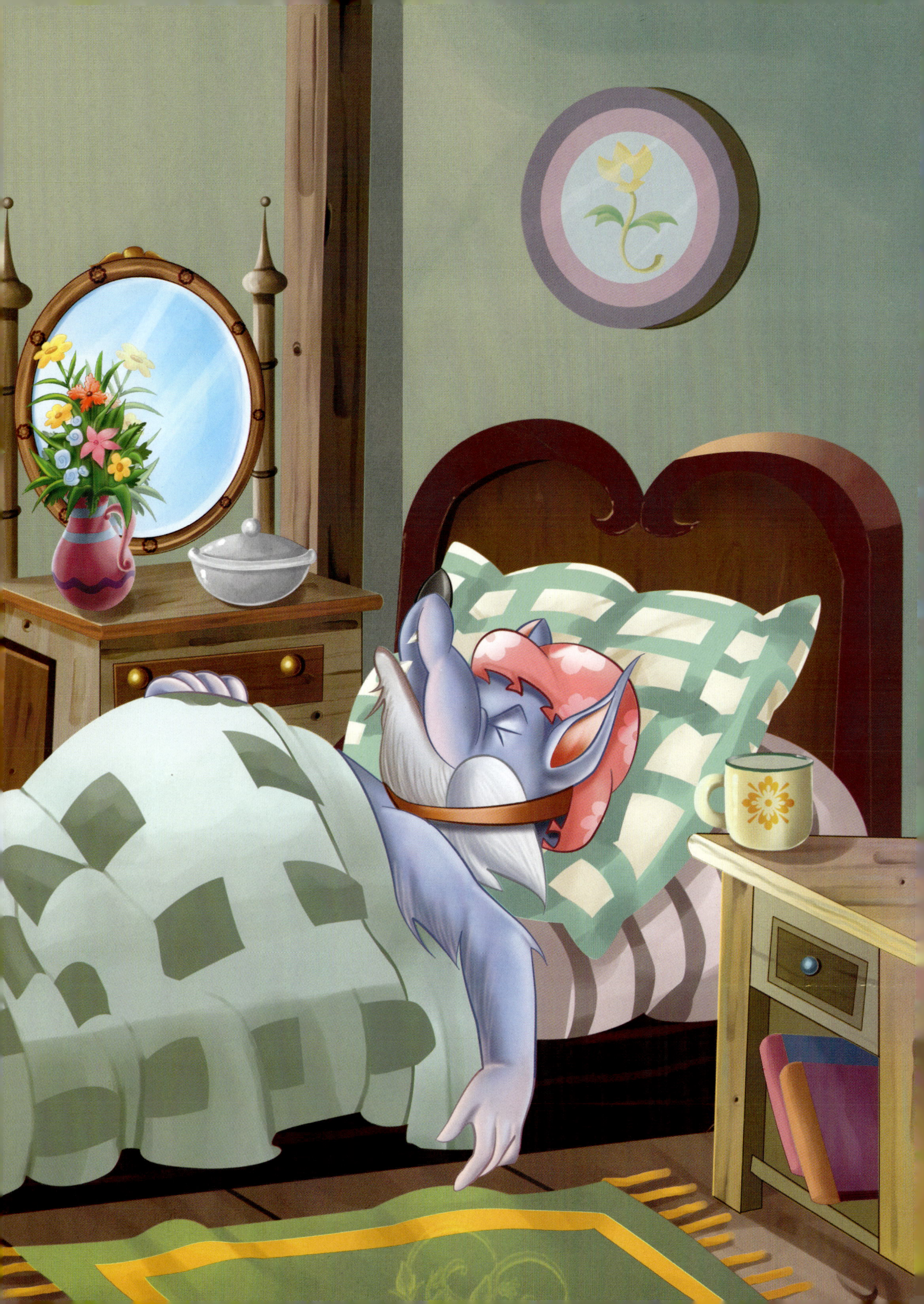

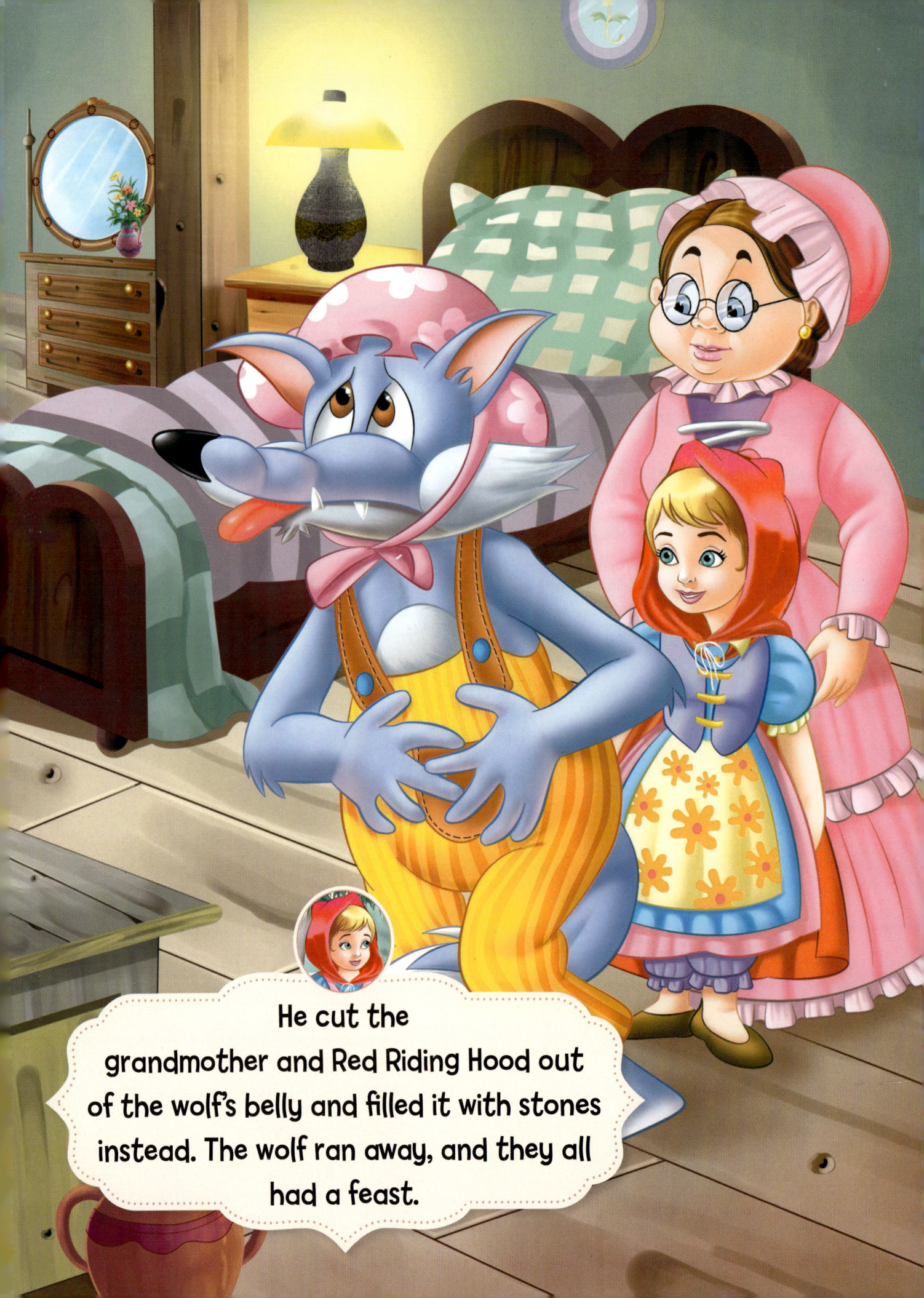

He cut the grandmother and Red Riding Hood out of the wolf's belly and filled it with stones instead. The wolf ran away, and they all had a feast.